BLOOD PETAL

A TALE OF REVENGE

MALVIKA CHATURVEDI

This book would not have been possible without the love
and support of my friends,family and honorable mentors.

Contents

Foreword

As a child i was always fascinated by fantasy,princesses,dungeons and dragons,and all dangerous stuff. When i learnt about the tale of the blood petal, i was eager to bring to life for my readers.

Preface

If you are sensitive, emotional or get scared easily, i would
advise you to stop reading this book immediately and bury
your thoughts into something more happy and jolly instead.
Good. Now that the strong ones have stayed, i would like
to warn you that this tale is wrapped in mystery, suspense,
horror and deceit

Acknowledgements

Dedicated to my beautiful dog Mylo. I will always and forever love you.

Prologue

When a great responsibility passes from generation to generation, it also brings a burden on the keeper. This is the story of a timeless magnificent rose, with blood petals hiding a tale of secrets from its keeper...

CHAPTER ONE

THE LAST KEEPER

It stood there—unwithered, untouched, and unbothered. As beautiful as ever, glowing as red as a burning ember. It seemed as if nothing had changed. Yet everything had.

Charlotte was now fifteen. She lived with her mother, Josephine, in a quaint, charming cottage that felt like something out of a fairy tale. But Charlotte was no ordinary girl. She had been chosen—the latest in a long line of keepers of the rose. A sacred role, entrusted to only one after millions before her.

Her father had died unexpectedly in the forest. Charlotte had always warned him to stay away, but he never listened. Until one day, he simply never returned.

But back to the rose. This was no ordinary flower. It was special. Magical. Both a blessing and a curse. Its power was immense. Used wisely, it could bring boundless happiness. Used recklessly, it could destroy the entire universe.

The long stemed red entity.

CHAPTER TWO

SHADOWS IN THE CELLAR

The next morning was far from pleasant. Charlotte's day began with her foot slipping into a puddle of ice-cold water. Trust me, that's not how you want to start your morning.

Her house was charming, but barely functional. It had drizzled all night and the water found its way inside through the cracks in the roof. She climbed out of bed and stood before the mirror, noticing a change she didn't like. Her face was paler than usual—no longer the radiant Charlotte she once was. She felt weak. Powerless. As if her purpose had drained away.

She made her way down to the cellar to water the rose. While she was making her way to the cellar, she realised she had something else she cherished down there—her father's memories. In a corroded storage chest lay a box full of his belongings: badges, letters, documents. But among all those relics, there was one treasure she held above all—a diary.

It was her father's diary, filled with his feelings and the details of that fateful day. She was about to open it when her mother's voice called from upstairs.

"Charlotte, breakfast is ready, darling!"

"Coming, Mother!"

Charlotte sighed deeply as she climbed the stairs. Only God knew what dark secrets that box was hiding.

Decaying metal box.

CHAPTER THREE

TORN BETWEEN WORLDS

Breakfast was heavy, weighed down by the thoughts of the diary swirling in Charlotte's mind.

"Mother, can I go back to the cellar?" she asked hesitantly.

"Sure, darling. Just don't hurt yourself," her mother replied, her voice tinged with an unfamiliar paranoia.

Down in the cellar, Charlotte's breath caught in her throat. Her eyes fell on a new entry in the diary that made her stomach drop into a bottomless pit.

Dear diary,

I have to hide the rose away from Charlotte. It has already caused too much destruction. I can't risk more harm to the universe. Charlotte is not ready, and if the rose falls into her hands, only God knows what will happen.

Her father never believed in her. He never truly thought she was ready to wield the rose's power.

Suddenly, a flood of questions crashed into her mind—Was it the rose that killed Father? Are there those who want to destroy it? If I am the chosen protector, then why me? Why now? Why here?

Overwhelmed, tears spilled down her cheeks as she hurried up the stairs.

Night fell, and Charlotte prepared for bed. Outside the window, the moon wasn't its usual pale white—it glowed a melancholic, crimson red. She barely noticed.

Just as sleep began to claim her, an unseen force gripped her—a surge of red energy pulling her from her bed. She clung desperately to the sheets, but it was no use.

And just like that, she vanished into the darkness of the night sky.

The diary

CHAPTER FOUR

BOUND BY THE ROSE

"Where am I?! Why did you bring me here?!" Charlotte cried, her voice breaking, but no one answered. Her screams dissolved into the thick obscurity surrounding her.

It felt like a basement, or maybe a closed graveyard—cold, dark, and suffocating. The feeling gnawed at her gut; she hated it.

An hour passed. Her fluttery pink floral dress was soaked through with tears. Just as she was gathering her strength to break free, a shadowy figure emerged.

Clad in a luxurious red velvet cape that shimmered faintly in the darkness, the figure approached. Beneath the cloak, a dress hinted at elegance and power.

Gently, the figure pulled back the hood, revealing the most beautiful woman Charlotte had ever seen.

"My name is Ophelia," she said, her British accent crisp and commanding. "I understand you are the keeper of the rose, and I've been told you have it."

She spoke with a forcefulness that brooked no argument. "I want it back."

"No," Charlotte said fiercely. "I am the keeper. I will do anything to protect it."

Ophelia smiled, cold and knowing. "Alright, Charlotte. Let's have it your way, then."

Suddenly, the ropes binding Charlotte to the chair tightened, cutting off her breath. She writhed, panic rising with every futile struggle.

Then, slowly, Ophelia loosened the ropes again.

"You see, darling," she whispered, leaning in close so her breath chilled Charlotte's ear, "I want that rose." Her voice was barely human—low, haunting.

"I'll give you all night to think about it—though you don't have much of a choice."

And with a twisted grin, she cackled into the darkness—an eerie sound that seemed to echo from the shadows themselves.

Ophelia

CHAPTER FIVE

THE KEEPER'S RESOLVE

Charlotte's breath came in shallow gasps as the ropes fell away, leaving her trembling—but defiant. The dim light flickered, casting long shadows that danced like specters across the room. Ophelia stood before her, an unsettling smile playing on her lips.

"You've made your choice," she murmured, her voice a velvet caress that sent a chill down Charlotte's spine. "But remember—every choice has its price."

With a swift motion, Ophelia extended her hand. The air grew heavy, thick with unseen force. Charlotte's vision blurred. The room pulsed, walls expanding and contracting like a living thing. A low, melodic hum filled the space, resonating deep in her chest.

"Do you feel it?" Ophelia's voice echoed—though her lips never moved. "The rose's power is awakening."

Suddenly, the ground beneath Charlotte gave way. She plunged into darkness.

Then, Ophelia's voice followed, calm and unnervingly cheerful:

"Now that I've shown you what I'm capable of, I suggest you surrender—and give me the rose."

"Never!" Charlotte shouted, her voice echoing through the void.

Ophelia laughed. "Alrighty then," she said, with unnerving enthusiasm.

Charlotte landed hard, knees buckling against cold stone. The darkness around her wasn't empty—it breathed. Whispered. Moved. She struggled to her feet, cradling her side where pain bloomed, but her grip on the rose tucked beneath her jacket remained firm.

A faint crimson glow pulsed from it now, barely illuminating the space. She didn't know why the rose had chosen her—or what it truly was—but it was the only thing keeping her grounded.

Above her, Ophelia's voice echoed again, soft and lilting. "You're strong, Charlotte. That's why the rose responded. But strength alone won't save you."

Charlotte clenched her jaw. "I don't need saving. Not by you."

The air shifted. Ophelia appeared, stepping from the shadows as though they parted willingly for her. Her smile was wider now, almost delighted. "You really think it's your choice? That you can keep it from me forever?"

Charlotte backed away slowly. The rose pulsed again—brighter this time. Warmer. Like it heard Ophelia's threat and rejected it.

"I won't give it up," Charlotte said. "I don't care what it costs me."

Ophelia tilted her head, eyes gleaming with something unreadable. "Oh, darling," she whispered. "That's exactly what I was hoping you'd say."

And with a snap of her fingers, the shadows surged.

Dark, cold and sad

CHAPTER SIX

THE FINAL PETAL

The shadows crashed down, and Charlotte hit the cold stone floor hard, the rose burning warm in her clenched fist. Pain flared in her ribs, but she forced herself up, breath shaky but steady.

Across the room, Ophelia stepped from the darkness, her usual confident smile cracked, uncertain.

"You don't even know what you're holding," she said softly. "That rose wasn't meant for someone like you."

Charlotte met her gaze, voice quiet but firm. "I don't want power. I just want to protect it—from people like you."

Ophelia's eyes darkened. "Power doesn't ask permission. It doesn't care about good or bad. It belongs to whoever takes it."

She raised her hands, and shadows whipped around the room like living storms. But the rose in Charlotte's palm flared bright—golden light spilling out, pushing the darkness back like the first light of dawn.

Charlotte's heart pounded as warmth spread through her. The rose wasn't just a weapon. It was a memory, a promise, a legacy of those who'd protected it before. Somwhere she could see her father holding the rose before her brimming with confidence.

"I didn't ask for this," Charlotte said, stepping forward. "But it chose me because I wouldn't use it to hurt."

Ophelia screamed and sent a spear of shadow crashing toward her.

Charlotte didn't flinch. She raised the rose, not as a sword, but like a beacon. Light wrapped around the spear, dissolving it. Then the shadows themselves began to unravel, peeling away like smoke in the morning sun.

Ophelia's scream turned to a whisper. "You could've ruled..."

Charlotte shook her head, tears stinging. "I'd rather be free."

And then, with a final burst of light, Ophelia vanished.

The room grew still. The rose's glow softened to a gentle pulse, a quiet heartbeat in Charlotte's palm.

She let out the breath she hadn't realized she was holding and smiled through the tears.

She hadn't won by overpowering darkness.

She'd won by refusing to become it.

The rose unweilding its power